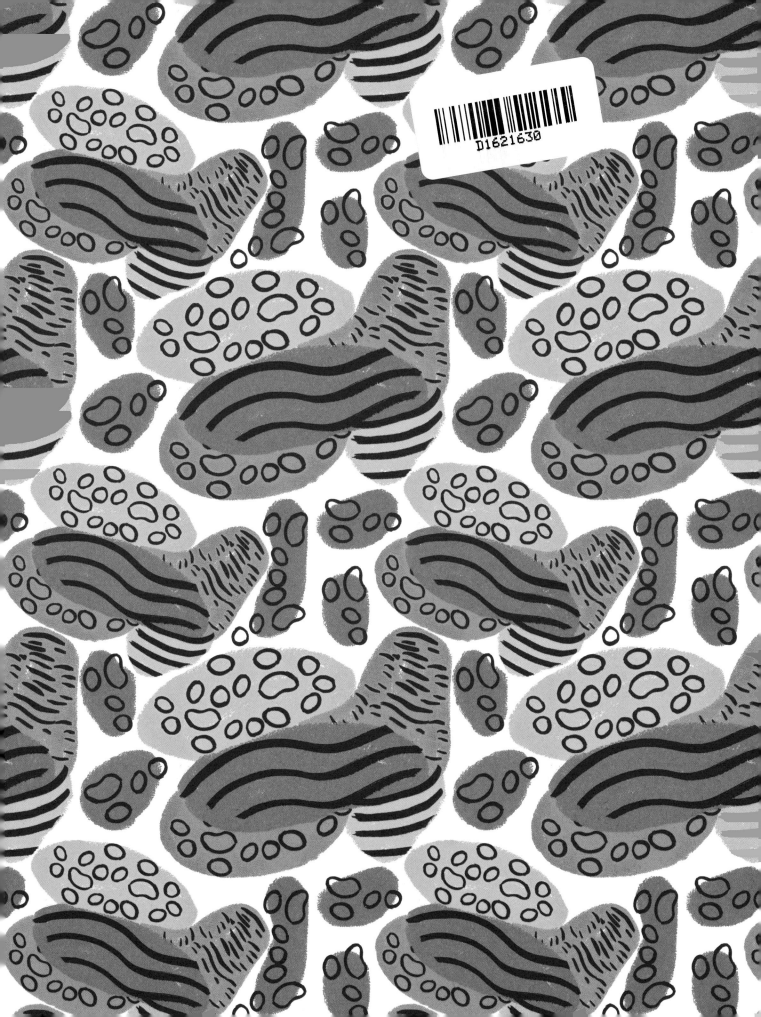

THIS BOOK BELONGS TO:

_____

_____

ICED out

WRITTEN
BY
CK SMOUHA

ILLUSTRATED
BY
ISABELLA
BUNNELL

Wilfred and Neville were not like the other kids in Miss Blubber's class.

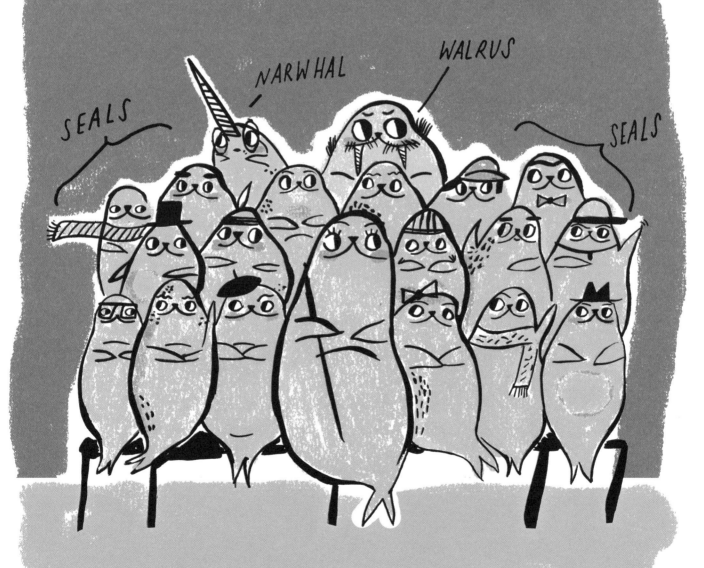

They never got picked for the soccer team.

Nobody wanted to sit next to them at lunchtime.

And at parties, they always seemed to ruin
the games...

...so they didn't get invited very often.

They didn't even like each other much.

Mornings were tough.

And Sundays were horrible.

One Monday, there was a new addition to
Miss Blubber's class.

And she was awesome.

At break, everyone wanted to play with her.
But Betty wasn't interested.

At lunchtime, everyone wanted to sit next to her.
But Betty preferred to sit alone.

She was amazing at soccer.
But didn't sign up for the team.

She got invited to all the parties.
But always seemed to have something better to do.

Wilfred and Neville were smitten.

Mornings were no longer a problem.

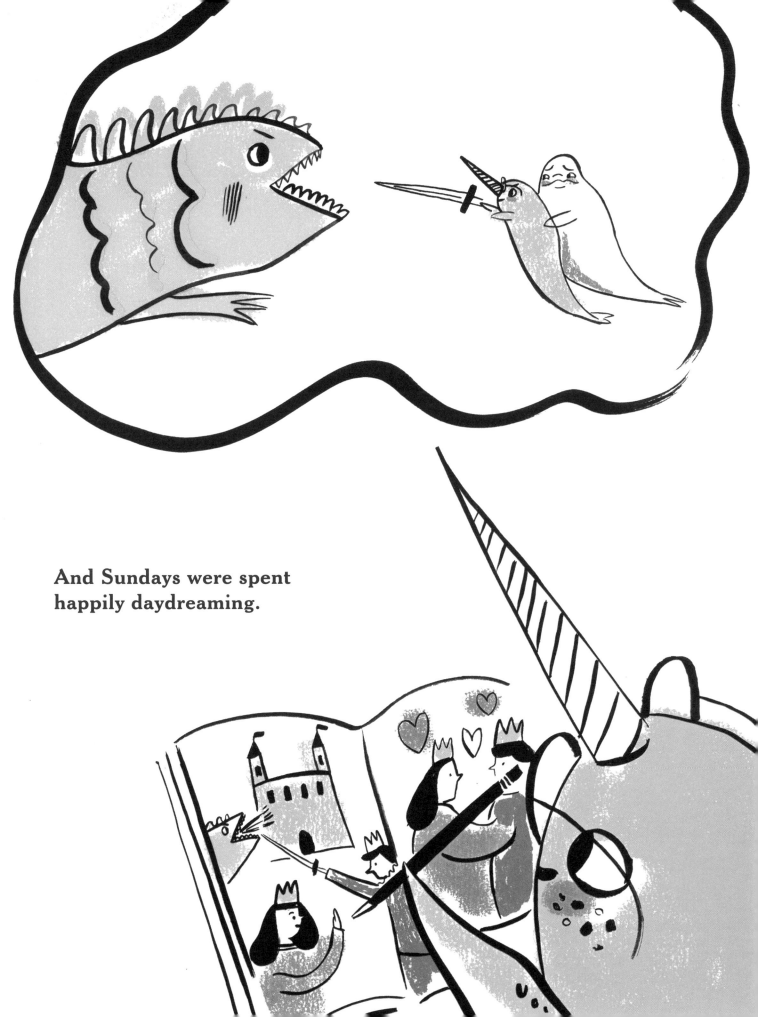

And Sundays were spent
happily daydreaming.

One day, Neville decided to take matters into his own hands.

He practiced.

And practiced.

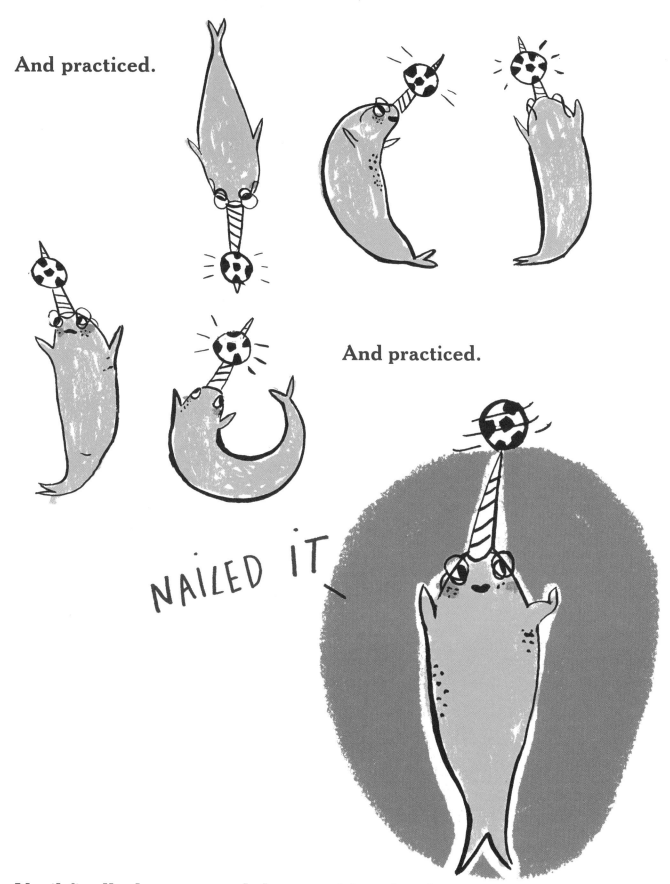

And practiced.

NAILED IT

Until finally, he mastered the one thing that he thought would always be beyond his reach.

At break, Neville swam purposefully up
to Betty.

But just as he got into position, it all went terribly wrong.

Neville was livid.

He searched high and low, but Wilfred was nowhere to be found.

Betty and Neville swam up and down looking for
Wilfred, to no avail.

Betty leaned against a big rock to catch her breath, and was surprised to find it was warm and rather hairy.

The three played hide-and-seek until home time.

It was glorious.

After they had cleared up a certain misunderstanding...

Wilfred, Neville and Betty became firm friends.

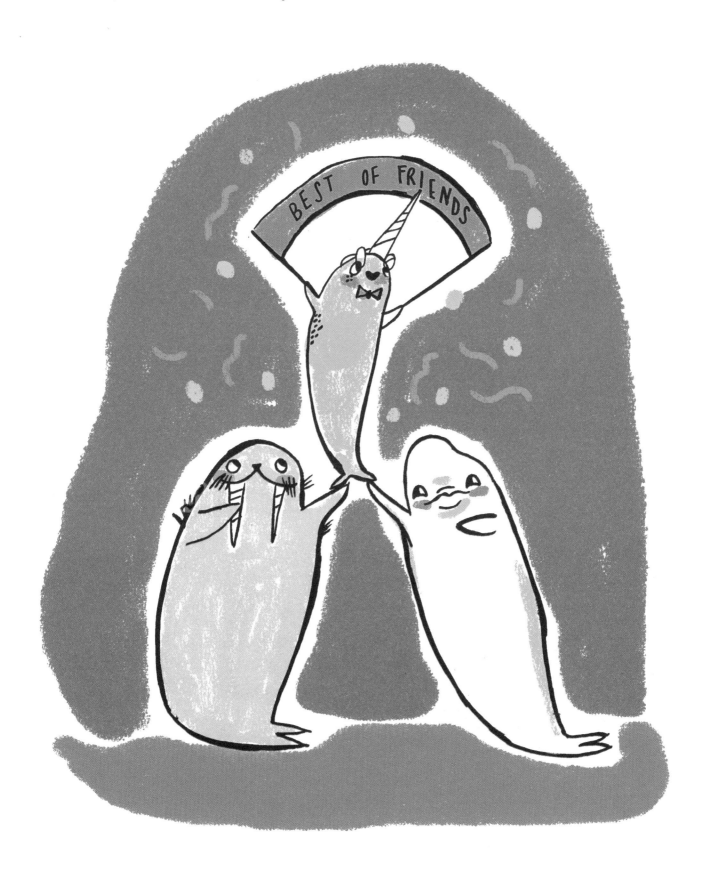

And everything changed.
Lunchtimes were fun.

And classwork was interesting.

Neville was still not great at soccer, but that was ok.

They even got invited to parties.

And sometimes, if they had nothing better to do, they would go.

Wilfred and Neville and Betty were not like the other kids in Miss Blubber's class.

And that was just fine.

ICED OUT

Written by C K Smouha
Illustrated by Isabella Bunnell

Designed by Alex Reece

British Library Cataloguing-in-Publication Data.
A CIP record for this book is available from the British Library.
ISBN: 978-1-908714-62-6

First published in 2019 by Cicada Books Ltd
© Cicada Books Limited

Printed in Poland

CG

Cicada Books Limited
48 Burghley Road
London NW5 1UE
www.cicadabooks.co.uk